Stellaluna

JANELL CANNON

Harcourt Brace & Company

SAN DIEGO   NEW YORK   LONDON

Copyright © 1993 by Janell Cannon

All rights reserved.
No part of this publication may be
reproduced or transmitted in any form or by any means,
electronic or mechanical, including photocopy, recording,
or any information storage and retrieval system, without
permission in writing from the publisher.

Requests for permission to make copies
of any part of the work should be mailed to
Permissions Department,
Harcourt Brace & Company, 8th Floor,
Orlando, Florida 32887.

Library of Congress Cataloging-in-Publication Data
Cannon, Janell, 1957–
Stellaluna/by Janell Cannon.
p.   cm.
Summary: After she falls headfirst
into a bird's nest, a baby bat is raised like a bird
until she is reunited with her mother.
ISBN 0-15-280217-7
1. Bats — Juvenile fiction.   2. Birds — Juvenile fiction.
[1. Bats — Fiction.   2. Birds — Fiction.]   I. Title
PZ10.3.C1685ST   1993
[E] — dc20   92-16439

F G

Printed in the United States of America

To
Burton H. Cannon
and
Nancy A. Cannon

With
Love

In a warm and sultry forest far, far away, there once lived a mother fruit bat and her new baby.

Oh, how Mother Bat loved her soft tiny baby. "I'll name you Stellaluna," she crooned.

Each night, Mother Bat would carry Stellaluna clutched to her breast as she flew out to search for food.

One night, as Mother Bat followed the heavy scent of ripe fruit, an owl spied her. On silent wings the powerful bird swooped down upon the bats.

Dodging and shrieking, Mother Bat tried to escape, but the owl struck again and again, knocking Stellaluna into the air. Her baby wings were as limp and useless as wet paper.

Down, down she went, faster and faster, into the forest below.

The dark leafy tangle of branches caught Stellaluna as she fell. One twig was small enough for Stellaluna's tiny feet. Wrapping her wings about her, she clutched the thin branch, trembling with cold and fear.

"Mother," Stellaluna squeaked. "Where are you?"

By daybreak, the baby bat could hold on no longer. Down, down again she dropped.

Flump! Stellaluna landed headfirst in a soft downy nest, startling the three baby birds who lived there.

Stellaluna quickly clambered from the nest and hung out of sight below it. She listened to the babble of the three birds.

"What was *that?*" cried Flap.

"I don't know, but it's hanging by its feet," chirped Flitter.

"Shhh! Here comes Mama," hissed Pip.

Many, many times that day Mama Bird flew away, always returning with food for her babies.

Stellaluna was terribly hungry — but *not* for the crawly things Mama Bird brought.

Finally, though, the little bat could bear it no longer. She climbed into the nest, closed her eyes, and opened her mouth.

Plop! In dropped a big green grasshopper!

Stellaluna learned to be like the birds. She stayed awake all day and slept at night. She ate bugs even though they tasted awful. Her bat ways were quickly disappearing. Except for one thing: Stellaluna still liked to sleep hanging by her feet.

Once, when Mama was away, the curious baby birds decided to try it, too. When Mama Bird came home she saw eight tiny feet gripping the edge of the nest.

"Eeeek!" she cried. "Get back up here this instant! You're going to fall and break your necks!"

The birds clambered back into the nest, but Mama Bird stopped Stellaluna. "You are teaching my children to do bad things. I will not let you back into this nest unless you promise to obey all the rules of this house."

Stellaluna promised. She ate bugs without making faces. She slept in the nest at night. And she didn't hang by her feet. Stellaluna behaved as a good bird should.

All the babies grew quickly. Soon the nest became crowded.

Mama Bird told them it was time to learn to fly. One by one, Pip, Flitter, Flap, and Stellaluna jumped from the nest.

Their wings worked!

I'm just like them, thought Stellaluna. I can fly, too.

Pip, Flitter, and Flap landed gracefully on a branch.
Stellaluna tried to do the same.

How embarrassing!

I will fly all day, Stellaluna told herself. Then no one will see how clumsy I am.

The next day, Pip, Flitter, Flap, and Stellaluna went flying far from home. They flew for hours, exercising their new wings.

"The sun is setting," warned Flitter.

"We had better go home or we will get lost in the dark," said Flap.

But Stellaluna had flown far ahead and was nowhere to be seen. The three anxious birds went home without her.

All alone, Stellaluna flew and flew until her wings ached and she dropped into a tree. "I promised not to hang by my feet," Stellaluna sighed. So she hung by her thumbs and soon fell asleep.

She didn't hear the soft sound of wings coming near.

"Hey!" a loud voice said. "Why are you hanging upside down?"

Stellaluna's eyes opened wide. She saw a most peculiar face. "I'm not upside down, *you* are!" Stellaluna said.

"Ah, but you're a *bat*. Bats hang by their feet. You are hanging by your thumbs, so that makes you *upside down!*" the creature said. "I'm a bat. I am hanging by my feet. That makes me *right side up!*"

Stellaluna was confused. "Mama Bird told me I was upside down. She said I was wrong . . ."

"Wrong for a bird, maybe, but not for a bat."

More bats gathered around to see the strange young bat who behaved like a bird. Stellaluna told them her story.

"You ate *b-bugs?*" stuttered one.

"You slept at *night?*" gasped another.

"How very strange," they all murmured.

"Wait! Wait! Let me look at this child." A bat pushed through the crowd. "An *owl* attacked you?" she asked. Sniffing Stellaluna's fur, she whispered, "You are *Stellaluna*. You are my baby."

"You escaped the owl?" cried Stellaluna. "You survived?"

"Yes," said Mother Bat as she wrapped her wings around Stellaluna. "Come with me and I'll show you where to find the most delicious fruit. You'll never have to eat another bug as long as you live."

"But it's nighttime," Stellaluna squeaked. "We can't fly in the dark or we will crash into trees."

"We're bats," said Mother Bat. "We can see in darkness. Come with us."

Stellaluna was afraid, but she let go of the tree and dropped into the deep blue sky.

Stellaluna *could* see. She felt as though rays of light shone from her eyes. She was able to see everything in her path.

Soon the bats found a mango tree, and Stellaluna ate as much of the fruit as she could hold.

"I'll never eat another bug as long as I live," cheered Stellaluna as she stuffed herself full. "I must tell Pip, Flitter, and Flap!"

The next day Stellaluna went to visit the birds.

"Come with me and meet my bat family," said Stellaluna.

"Okay, let's go," agreed Pip.

"They hang by their feet and they fly at night and they eat the best food in the world," Stellaluna explained to the birds on the way.

As the birds flew among the bats, Flap said, "I feel upside down here."

So the birds hung by their feet.

"Wait until dark," Stellaluna said excitedly. "We will fly at night."

When night came Stellaluna flew away. Pip, Flitter, and Flap leapt from the tree to follow her.

"I can't see a thing!" yelled Pip.

"Neither can I," howled Flitter.

"Aaeee!" shrieked Flap.

"They're going to crash," gasped Stellaluna. "I must rescue them!"

Stellaluna swooped about, grabbing her friends in the air. She lifted them to a tree, and the birds grasped a branch. Stellaluna hung from the limb above them.

"We're safe," said Stellaluna. Then she sighed. "I wish you could see in the dark, too."

"We wish you could land on your feet," Flitter replied. Pip and Flap nodded.

They perched in silence for a long time.

"How can we be so different and feel so much alike?" mused Flitter.

"And how can we feel so different and be so much alike?" wondered Pip.

"I think this is quite a mystery," Flap chirped.

"I agree," said Stellaluna. "But we're friends. And that's a fact."

BAT NOTES

Of the nearly 4,000 species of mammals on Earth, almost one quarter are bats, the only mammals capable of powered flight.

The scientific name for bats is Chiroptera, "hand-wing," because the skeleton that supports the wing is composed of the animal's elongated finger bones.

The majority of bats are classified as Microchiroptera, "small hand-wing." Nearly 800 varieties fill special niches in every climate around the world except the polar zones. The lifestyles and food preferences of Microchiroptera vary widely. Many eat insects, while others catch fish, amphibians, and reptiles. Finally, there is the famous vampire, of which there are only three species, ranging from Mexico to Argentina. The vampire's victims are mostly domestic cattle and native mammals and birds.

The other 170 or so species of bats are the fruit bats, otherwise known as Megachiroptera, or "large hand-wing." As their name implies, these are the largest bats, some types boasting wingspans of six feet.

Fruit bats generally have long muzzles, large eyes, pointy ears, and furry bodies, which is why they are often called flying foxes. Unlike the Microchiroptera, who travel by echolocation, fruit bats depend on their keen vision and sense of smell to navigate. They live in tropical and subtropical climates that provide year-round supplies of their favorite fruit, flowers, and nectar. Some fruit bats, as they forage for nectar, are responsible for pollination of many types of night-blooming trees and plants. Others eat whole fruits, seeds and all, and distribute the seeds over the forest floor in their droppings. Regeneration of tropical forests depends greatly on bats.

The illustrations in this book were done in
Liquitex acrylics and Prismacolor pencils on bristol board.
The display type was hand-lettered by Judythe Sieck.
The text type was set in Guardi #55 by Thompson Type, San Diego, California.
Color separations by Bright Arts, Ltd., Singapore
Printed by The Eusey Press, Leominster, Massachusetts
Bound by The Book Press, Brattleboro, Vermont
Production supervision by Warren Wallerstein and Ginger Boyer
Designed by Trina Stahl

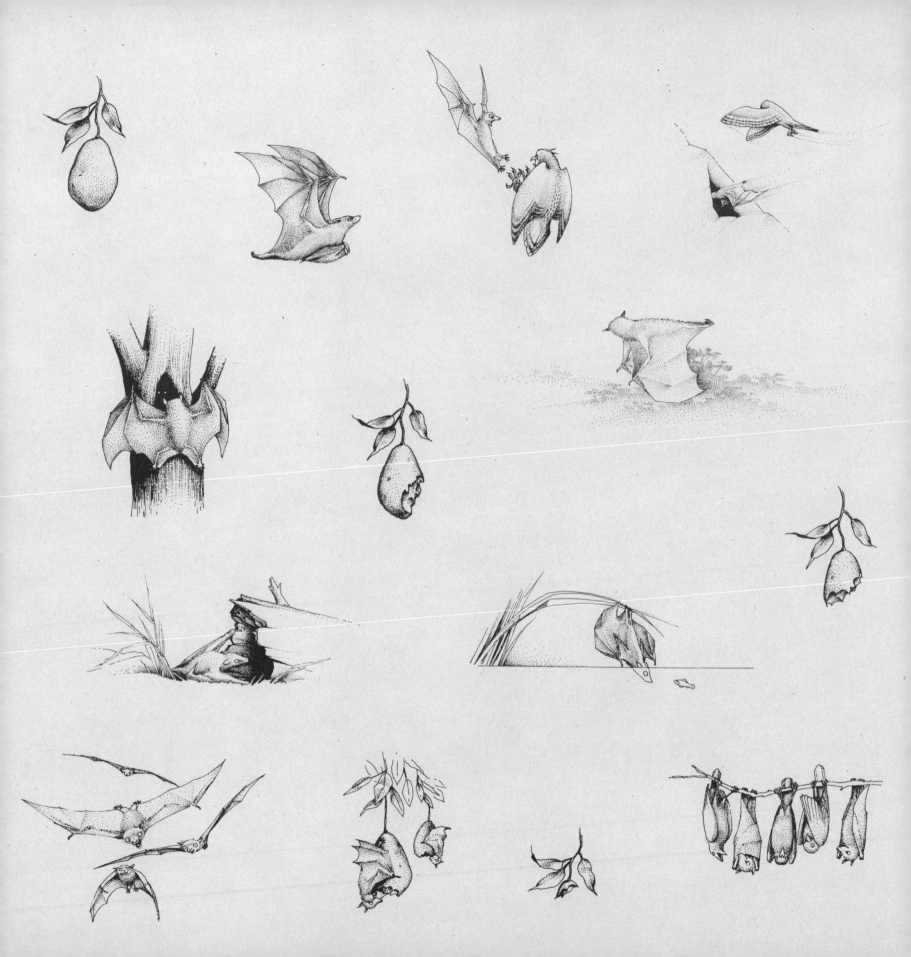